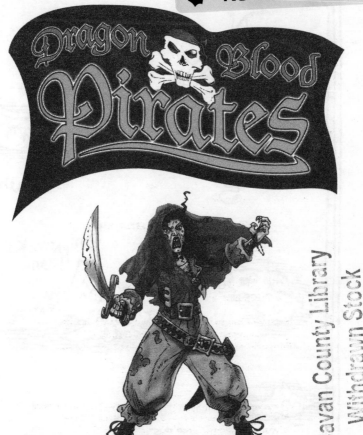

Dragon Blood Pirates

The Evil Pearl

Dan Jerris

ORCHARD BOOKS

For Emily, the just

/E)

www.dragonbloodpirates.co.uk

ORCHARD BOOKS
338 Euston Road, London NW1 3BH

First published in 2008 by Lothian Children's Books,
an imprint of Hachette Livre Australia
First published in the UK in 2011 by Orchard Books

ISBN 978 1 40830 826 4

Text © Dan Jerris 2009
Skull, crossbones and ragged parchment image © Brendon De Suza
Map illustrations on pages 4–5 © Rory Walker, 2008
All other illustrations © Orchard Books 2011

A CIP catalogue record for this book is available from the British Library.

10 9 8 7 6 5 4 3 2 1

Printed in Great Britain

Orchard Books is a division of Hachette Children's Books,
an Hachette UK company.

www.hachette.co.uk

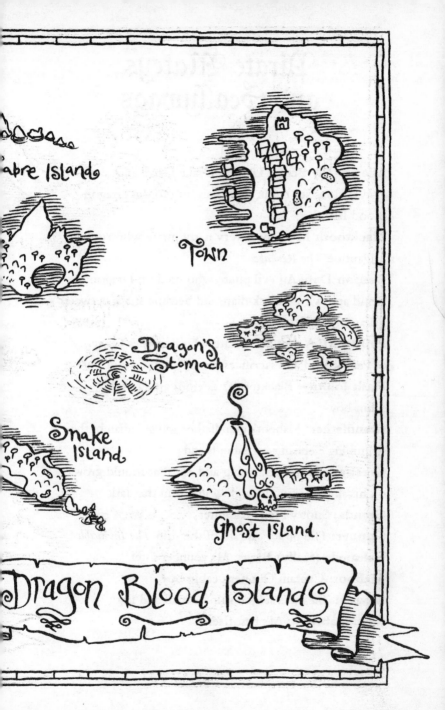

abre Island

Town

Dragon's Stomach

Snake Island

Ghost Island.

Dragon Blood Islands

Pirate Mateys and Scallywags

Alleric (Al) Breas: Lives in Drake Drive and owns a mysterious sea trunk that takes him to the Dragon Blood Islands

Blacktooth McGee: A very nasty pirate who runs the brigantine *The Revenge*

Demon Dan: An evil pirate who died on Dragon Island and whose black diamond became stuck between a dragon's teeth

Evil Pearl: A deathless pirate who becomes Queen of Pearl Island and sacrifices people to a sea monster

Flash Johnny: Blacktooth's devious and greedy cabin boy

Grandfather: Mahoot's grandfather and guardian of the swimming elephants on Sabre Island

Greeny Joe: A shark so big and old that mould grows on his skin, making him glow green in the dark

Grenda: Snotty Nell's daughter

Gunner: The pirate captain of the ship *The Invincible*

Halimeda (Hally) Breas: Al's younger sister

Mahoot: Captain Gunner's cabin boy

Mozzy: *The Invincible*'s bosun – small and fast

Jack Seabrook: Al's best friend

Pigface McNurt: Blacktooth's bosun; a huge pirate with a ring through his nose

Prince Alleric: The prince who once ruled Sabre Island but disappeared in mysterious circumstances

Princess Haree: The princess of Ruby Island

Razor Toe: A deathless pirate who has enslaved the people of Ruby Island

Sharkbait: Snotty Nell's one-legged bosun

Slicer: *The Invincible's* cook

Snakeboot: A magical white three-legged cat with purple eyes. Legend has it he once belonged to a terrifying pirate called Vicious Victor.

Snotty Nell: A horrible one-eyed pirate who sails a worn-out Indiaman called *Nausi VIII*

Stanley Spong: A crooked, sneaky trader in town who cheats people

Vampire Zu: Snotty Nell's huge first mate

Velvetfoot: A fearsome pirate distinctive for his velvet shoes that let him creep up on his victims unannounced

Vicious Victor: A pirate ghost. He used to pillage the Dragon Blood Islands and stole the magical sabre and scabbard that belonged to Prince Alleric.

The Magic Ring

"What do you mean, my ring's magic?" asked Hally, inspecting a dragon-headed ring set with a pearl in its mouth.

"Your ring was made by the same sorcerer who made the Scabbard of Invincibility and the Dragon Blood Sabre," her brother, Al, explained.

"And we really need you to lend it to us for a few hours," said Al's best friend, Jack. "We're not actually sure it is magic."

"Well, is it or not?" asked Hally. "I'm confused."

"We found out about your ring from a book in Alleric Castle," Al tried to explain. "*My* ring had magical powers, but that pirate kid, Flash, stole it. So come on, let's borrow yours. You're not using it."

"Hang on a minute," said Hally. "You want to take my ring to the Dragon Blood Islands but leave me behind? I don't think that's very fair."

"But you don't like sailing," argued Jack.

Al winced at Jack's words. Hally didn't like being told what she didn't like.

"I didn't know my ring was magic," said Hally. "Besides, I haven't played princesses for ages. I might want to come with you."

"What if we're captured by Blacktooth or Snotty Nell?" Jack shuddered at the thought of how horrible they were.

"You're just a little girl who gets scared,"

said Al. He quickly regretted his words as Hally stamped her foot and her eyes flared.

"I am not just a little girl," she said. "I don't always get scared, and you're not getting rid of me that easily!"

"We're not trying to get rid of you," said Al. "All we want to do is see if your ring can help us find another black diamond for the Scabbard of Invincibility. We've got two already, but we think Vicious Victor gave us

your ring on purpose, to help us in
our quest."

"In that case," argued Hally, "since that
ghostly old pirate gave the ring to me,
I think he wanted me to use it. And that
means I should come with you."

"Well, I suppose you can come then, if
you're brave enough," said Al, giving in. "But
you've got ten minutes to get ready, and if
you're not in the attic by then, we're going
without you."

When Al and Jack got to the attic they
changed into their pirate clothes, unlocked
the old sea trunk with an iron key and were
about to step inside when Hally appeared
at the door. She wore a long, old-fashioned
dress and the pearl ring was glowing on
her finger.

"Why aren't you wearing your scabbard
and sabre?" she asked her brother.

"Because the pirates want them," said Al. "I'm leaving them here so they can't chase us for them."

"You're not scared, are you?" mocked Hally. "You're not just a little girl?"

"I'm not scared," Al snapped. "I'm just being sensible."

"Well, I'm brave," said Hally, "and you're not!"

"Fine, I'll wear them then," said Al, pulling a dazzling silver scabbard inlaid with two enormous black diamonds from a cupboard, along with a golden sabre with a large ruby in the handle. He placed the sabre in the scabbard and strapped it to his waist.

"Well, Prince Alleric, you do look fine,"

teased Hally in her princess voice. "Now I'm ready to go to the Dragon Blood Islands. Lead the way."

Al wished someone would pour cold water on his sister's silly ideas.

"Where are we headed this time?" asked Jack as Al stepped into the trunk.

Before Al could think of an answer he and his companions shimmered, became transparent and vanished from the twenty-first century and the house at number five Drake Drive.

Watery Landing

Al found himself plummeting into the ocean. He kicked desperately for the surface and, seconds later, Jack popped up beside him, eyes round with shock.

Hally, too, struggled above water, gasping for air, and swam towards her brother. "Al!" she cried. "How come we're in the sea?"

"I don't know," replied Al, treading water to stay afloat, remembering his silly wish. "I just stepped into the trunk without thinking."

Jack looked around wildly. "We're way out in the ocean. There's not even an island nearby."

"And I can't swim very well," Hally whimpered. "What if we drown?"

"It's OK, we can hold on to the scabbard," said Al. "As long as we do that we can't die."

"But, remember, we can never let go of the black diamonds or we'll die instantly," said Jack. "The black diamonds make you deathless. So, even if we died we'd be strangely alive…"

Hally began to sob. "I should've stayed home!"

"We should float on our backs and hold hands so we don't get separated," said Al, trying to calm his sister. "We've got to save our strength to stay alive."

The children floated for several minutes, but soon their heavy clothes began to drag them down. "I wish there was something to hold me up," Hally wailed, struggling against the folds of her dress.

Al lifted his head to search the ocean for something that might give them support or help, and his eyes caught a movement about a hundred metres away. A fin! He shut his eyes and tried not to panic. Somewhere he'd read that sharks were attracted to violent movements and sound. He didn't think he should make matters worse by telling the others they were about to be eaten alive.

He opened his eyes again, hoping the fin would have gone away, but it was moving ever closer. Worse, several more were cutting the water further out. Now there were at least six sharks. He shut his eyes again. Black diamonds or not, they were doomed!

Something nudged his leg and a terrified shout escaped his lips. Hally and Jack looked around and, seeing the fins so close, also screamed in panic.

Then, a dark shape moved right beside Al's head. There was a sudden whoosh of air and he was lifted from the ocean. After his initial horror, Al realised with a surge of relief that it was just a dolphin, pushing him!

One by one the other friendly creatures swam up to the children.

"They're helping us!" cried Hally, as they were gently pushed along.

The dolphins took it in turns to lift the children and stop them sinking. Feeling more confident, Al reached out and held on to a dorsal fin. "Grab their fins," he told the others. "They might tow us."

To their delight, the children found themselves travelling through the ocean on the backs of a pod of dolphins, until they came across a dead tree bobbing in the waves. When the trio clambered onto the floating wood, their rescuers swam away.

"I wish I could thank them," said Hally, and in an instant the dolphins returned, nudging her with their noses.

"Thank you," said Hally, patting each dolphin's head. In turn, each creature squeaked, flipped its tail, did a wonderful somersault and was gone.

Alone again, at first the children felt quite safe, but as the day wore on the log became unbearably uncomfortable and Hally started to grumble and complain. The bobbing swells took them nowhere and, by afternoon, the churning ocean and chilling breeze had truly exhausted her. She sat silently with the others, watching the horizon.

Just before dark, when the children thought they'd never see human life again, the sails of a ship appeared, tacking in their direction.

"It's the *Nausi VIII*," said Al, recognising the wallowing boat as it came closer.

"Not Snotty's ship!" groaned Jack. "She hates us!"

"And she'll probably steal the sabre and scabbard," said Al, regretting that he'd ever brought them back.

"And my ring," said Hally. "I'd better hide it in my pocket."

"I can't hide the sabre," said Al, "but maybe she'll be nicer than usual because we saved her life last time we were here."

And so, despite their fear of Snotty Nell, the children, exhausted by the ocean, waved and called out to attract attention.

Mermaid Island

The dripping children were soon standing before Snotty Nell. "What are you lot doing out here?" she asked, her one good eye never leaving Al's sabre and scabbard. "Gunner's ship hasn't sunk by any miracle?"

"No," answered Jack. "He's still sailing *The Invincible*."

"We weren't with Gunner," explained Al. "We were playing and just got caught by the ocean."

"But some dolphins rescued us," said Hally.

"And pigs might fly, Hally," snorted Snotty.

"Princess Halimeda to you," Hally corrected, annoyed at being called a liar.

Snotty stiffened at her words, but turned on Al. "You're wearing something that little boys don't deserve to have." She wiped her nose on her sleeve and held out her hand for the sabre and scabbard. "I heard they'd been found but I didn't believe it. Give them to me and I won't feed you to the fishes."

"What are you going to do with them?" asked Al as he reluctantly unbuckled the scabbard and sabre and held them out to Snotty.

"Learn how to use the sabre's magic," said Snotty, pulling the weapon from its sheath and waving it through the air, "and tomorrow I'll dump you on Mermaid Island when we stop for water."

"Are there mermaids there?" asked Hally.

"Of course there are, dear," said Snotty,

with a smirk that twisted her scarred face. "And they're expecting a princess for morning tea."

"Does it have a town?" asked Al, wondering how he was going to get his scabbard and sabre back.

Snotty shook her head. "Deserted. And now that I've saved your life, I don't owe you a thing. We're even. So don't you go bringing up how you stopped that dragon from eating me."

"I wasn't going to," said Al, "but I was hoping for a bit more than being abandoned on an island."

"Well, as you so kindly gave me this wonderful sabre, I'll give you some provisions," said Snotty. "Now it's off to the brig with you."

As Al, Jack and Hally moved from earshot, Snotty turned to her first mate, Vampire Zu. "Take them below and keep watch on them.

They're trouble. I don't trust them to be left on their own for a second. And don't tell my daughter they're on board. They have a habit of turning her soft."

The following morning Vampire Zu and a small crew of pirates collected the children from the brig, lowered them into a longboat and rowed them ashore. Once on the beach the pirates clambered out.

"While we're collecting water you can

unload your supplies," said Vampire Zu, pointing to a tarpaulin at the stern of the longboat. He glanced up at the sky and signalled to his brigands to unload the water barrels. "We'd better hurry, mateys. There's a storm coming. Snotty's on a bad anchor."

As the pirates left, Al moved to the back of the longboat and pulled back the tarpaulin. He jumped when a voice said, "I bet you didn't expect to see me!"

"Grenda!" cried Al, as a girl peered out from between their supplies.

"What are you doing here?" said Jack, smiling at Snotty's daughter.

"I saw you being rescued from a porthole and I sneaked up and listened," said Grenda. "Mum wouldn't let me talk to you. When I said I would anyway, she locked me in my cabin, but I had a spare key."

"She'll have your guts for garters," said Jack in admiration.

"I'll sneak back to my cabin before she misses me," said Grenda.

"You're brilliant," Al said with a smile.

"Well, you've saved Mum's life twice now, so I wanted you to know that as soon as we get back to town I'll leave a message for Captain Gunner and he can come to get you."

"Thanks, Grenda," said Jack. "You're brave going against your mum."

Grenda shrugged off the praise. "I really only stowed away because I wanted to see mermaids."

"There might be some up by those rocks," said Hally, pointing along the beach.

"Let's have a quick look," said Grenda. "We won't be long."

As the two girls ran off, Al and Jack began unloading their supplies. They had only been working for a short time when the wind suddenly turned and blew onshore. Vampire Zu and his men re-appeared unexpectedly early, hurrying along the beach.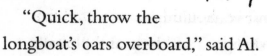

"Grenda's not back yet," said Jack, watching them approach. "How can we slow them down?"

"Quick, throw the longboat's oars overboard," said Al.

This only made the pirates angry and in seconds the oars were gathered and set back in their rowlocks.

"You can't go," cried Al, throwing himself into the boat. "It's too soon. You haven't filled all your water barrels."

"I'll skewer yer gizzard if you try that again," growled Vampire Zu, grabbing Al by the waist and throwing him into the water.

"No!" shouted Jack, rushing to the longboat and grabbing it with both hands.

"We haven't finished unloading. At least you could help us. How can you leave us behind without enough food?"

"Get away with you, you scurvy dogs!" roared Vampire. "If I had my way, I'd slit your rotten throats." With those words the pirates clambered into the longboat and rowed away.

"Maybe we should have admitted that Grenda was here," said Jack, as the pirates disappeared over the rising swell. "It might have been better than having them leave without her."

Al nodded. "I know. I didn't want to tell on her, but this is worse. We made a mess of it. I'm going to feel awful when Hally and Grenda get back."

The storm blew up and huge waves smashed onto the beach, making any return of the *Nausi VIII* impossible.

"Mum'll be really worried," moaned Grenda when she and Hally returned to the boys. "The storm's so fierce, she might think I fell overboard."

"We tried to stop them leaving," said Al. "I'm sorry."

"And I'm sorry we didn't see any mermaids," said Hally. "I wish there were a few around. They might be able to show us some shelter or a way to get out of here."

"What's that?" asked Jack suddenly, pointing at something in the surf.

Al blinked through the rain. A mermaid-like tail splashed – but then a large creature slowly emerged from the sea. It waddled cautiously towards them.

"It's a funny-looking, fat-headed seal," said Hally. "It's like an ugly old woman."

"It's a dugong," explained Jack. "Sailors used to call them mermaids."

"I thought mermaids were supposed to

be beautiful," said Grenda. "This one looks hideous."

"Isn't it true that dugongs never leave the water?" said Al, as the beast stopped in front of Hally.

"Well, looks like this one must be keen on Hally, then," said Jack, suppressing a giggle.

The dugong reared up and chirped in a strange voice.

"What does she want?" asked Grenda.

"I don't know, but I wish she could show us some shelter," said Hally. "I'm sick of being wet and cold."

At her words the creature waved her flipper in the air.

"I know this is weird," said Al, "but I think she's beckoning. Maybe she's asking us to follow her."

When Al moved towards her, the creature shuffled backwards. The children followed as she lumbered along the beach. Finally

she stopped and signalled with her flipper,
pointing up to the sand dunes.

"Are you telling us to go up there?" asked
Hally.

The dugong nodded her gigantic head,
turned and shuffled back into the water.

"We should at least go and look where she
pointed," suggested Al, watching the strange
creature swim away.

"Did you notice she came just after Hally
wished a mermaid would help us?" said Jack.
"Could that be a coincidence?"

"Perhaps my ring really is magic," said
Hally.

"The dolphins came when you wished we
could float in the ocean, too," said Jack.

"What ring?" asked Grenda.

Hally reached into a fold in her dress and
pulled out her precious jewellery. "This one,"
she said. "I hid it from your mum."

"It might be a wishing ring," said Al.

"You'd better wish that you have more than three wishes."

"And tuck it away somewhere safe," said Grenda.

After several minutes of searching the dunes, Al discovered an oar. Shortly afterwards Jack trod on something that echoed under his feet. Everyone started digging and they uncovered a wooden dory with its mast and sails carefully stowed along its hull. It didn't take long for them to tip the rowboat onto its side and use it to shelter from the lashing winds.

"We can sail out of here once the weather improves," said Al. "What a fantastic find!"

Meanwhile, as Snotty waited for Vampire Zu to return with the water, she locked herself in her cabin and inspected her legendary treasures. She admired the two black diamonds on the Scabbard of Invincibility, thinking they would make a lovely pair of earrings. She strapped the scabbard to her waist and removed the famous Dragon Blood Sabre. Her eye sparkled with delight at the wonderful ruby in the hilt.

Now if I remember correctly, she thought, *legend says that Prince Alleric could fly anywhere with this sabre, just like a magic-carpet ride.* She waved the sabre through the air and wished to be in a prince's castle, so she could steal some jewels. She shut her eyes. Nothing happened. She tried again.

"Stupid thing," she muttered, shaking the sabre. "Maybe I'm not waving it hard enough." Using all her strength she slashed the sabre through the air. At the same time the boat pitched violently in the rising swell.

The sharp sabre whipped downwards with more force than Snotty had expected, slashing into her thigh and cutting it deeply. Shocked, she dropped the sabre and bent

over, clutching her
bleeding wound.

"Help!" she
screamed. "Help!"

Sharkbait,
her one-legged
bosun, heard the
cries and limped over
to her cabin. Realising the cabin door was
locked, he grabbed a blunderbuss and fired
at the catch.

"Arrrghh!" shrieked Snotty, as splinters
hurtled into her bottom. "You scurvy
blowfish, I'll have you keelhauled!"

Sharkbait leapt into the cabin and, seeing
Snotty injured, ran for the medicine chest. As
he tended to the gash in Snotty's leg, the ship
pitched furiously on its anchor and Snotty
glared miserably at the scabbard and sabre.
The storm shook the rigging, but finally
the grinding of a winch told Snotty that

Vampire Zu had returned and was stowing the longboat.

Rubbing her tender spots, she hobbled onto the deck and, seeing the raging sea and the white water all around them, supervised the *Nausi VIII*'s departure from Mermaid Island.

Once they were under sail again, Snotty left Vampire Zu at the helm and returned to her cabin. She threw herself on her bunk and began to pull splinters from her rump with a pair of tweezers.

While the ship rolled and wallowed in the breeze, Snotty, feeling very grumpy, threw the sabre and scabbard into the corner of her cabin. "Fakes," she cried. "They're obviously fakes. How could that stinking scabbard make anyone invincible? Just look at my horrible wounds! And I bet the diamonds are glass! Who ever heard of black diamonds? Those horrible children have had a big joke at my expense!"

Only when she had stopped feeling sorry for herself did Snotty limp down to Grenda's cabin. Finding it empty, she thought one of the other pirates had probably let her out, but when Grenda didn't come for supper Snotty began to worry. She searched the *Nausi VIII* from bilge to crow's nest. Finally she panicked.

She ordered the ship be turned about and sailed into the storm. Lashed by wind and rain, the one-eyed pirate stood at the helm.

"Grenda!" she cried out, sobbing, watching every tossing wave. "Grenda!"

The Galleon

Two days later, with no sign of Snotty Nell, the castaways launched the dory and it flew before the breeze.

That night at sea, Al volunteered for first watch. Shortly before the moon rose, a change in the movement of the water alerted him that something wasn't quite right. He stared into the darkness, watching for danger. Under the faint starlight he finally made out the shape of an enormous galleon rolling towards them in the swells.

"Help!" he called, surprised that such a large ship had drifted so close unnoticed. His cry woke the others who, seeing the ship, joined in, shouting for attention, but the galleon only creaked and groaned in reply.

"There are no ship lights and no sails," said Grenda. "It's spooky."

"It's dragging a line," Jack pointed out. "We could tie it up and climb aboard."

"We'd be safer on a big boat than a little one," Hally agreed. "We could sleep there instead of the dory. But I can't climb a rope."

"Jack and I will go aboard and we'll lower a ladder or something if it's safe," said Al. He grabbed the trailing rope, wrapped his legs and arms around it and monkeyed upwards. Jack followed.

When both the girls were hauled aboard

and the dory was secure, they began to look around.

"Hello!" Al yelled. His voice carried away to silence. "I don't think there's anyone aboard," he said, "but we'd better be careful, just in case. Let's go to bed here, and we can explore in the morning when it's light."

Exhausted, Jack, Hally and Grenda didn't disagree. They lay down where they were and went to sleep.

At first light, they discovered that the deck was littered with bird droppings and the ropes on the masts were disintegrating.

"Let's go below and explore," said Grenda.

The main hatch was locked fast, so Al found a belaying pin and used it to force the hatch open. They scrambled down some ancient, rotting stairs. The timbers dripped moisture and mould squelched under their feet as they crept warily down the companionway. But soon a dark shape blocked their way.

Al leant towards it cautiously and then jumped back. "Don't look," he warned. "It's disgusting."

But Grenda was intrigued and she too bent down, staring at the shape. "Yuck!" she said. "Mouldy bones in slime. Do you think someone died in a battle for riches?"

"We could check the treasure room," suggested Jack.

As they explored the warren of passageways, they glimpsed other skeletons lying slumped in their hammocks or sitting at tables.

"It's weird," said Jack. "They don't look like they've been in a fight. It's more like they died where they were, frozen in time."

They soon discovered the treasure room, but it was empty.

"Let's find the captain's cabin," said Al, shivering slightly in the gloom. "As they say, dead men tell no tales, but someone might have kept a record or something."

"Follow me," said Grenda, leading them upwards to the stern of the boat until they found themselves in a grand cabin. The ship's logbook lay untouched on the captain's table. Al opened it at the last entry and read aloud:

I, the first mate of this treasure galleon, write these pages. And woe is me, for my black heart and that of my captain has caused our fate.

On a small island, peopled by gentle folk, we heard of a temple with a treasure trove of pearls, dedicated to the god of the sea. We made our way through the village to reach it, broke down the temple doors and murdered every monk to get to the booty.

The chief abbot fell upon the pearls, protecting them with his body, but our captain stabbed him. With his dying breath the abbot cursed us: "The god of the sea will be avenged!

*Death more
painful
than mine
is yours, and
for every pearl
you steal, a pearl
of pain ye shall bear
until your lives be taken."*

Laughing at the curse, our captain took the treasure and we sailed away. Two days out, the captain collapsed with pain throughout her body. Boils burst out upon her face and arms. Each one grew to the size of a walnut, then to that of a hen's egg, and caused exceeding pain. The sickness lasted three days, and on the fourth she vomited blood. This continued for three days, there being no means of healing it.

But the curse was amongst us all and the outbreak of death began. Soon corpses lay in their hammocks or where they fell, for no one dared touch them.

One night, deathly ill and insane from pain, our captain staggered to the treasure room. She single-handedly managed to pull out the cursed chest of pearls and drag it onto the deck. At the ship's longboat she slumped across her evil treasure, and lay without movement for many days.

The sun beat down, but she would neither rot nor stink. Finally, those still alive could stand it no more and went to throw her body overboard but, to our horror, the woman stood! Alive but dead! Wielding her sword, and with her face and arms covered in pearls stuck to her sore-ridden flesh, she shouted, "I will live and I will give the sea god what is due!"

Terrified of such evil, we locked ourselves below decks. Trapped with the dead, we listened as our captain walked the deck.

Finally, in the second week, our boat drifted back to the island of the sea god. With land in sight, our captain lowered the longboat and rowed ashore, taking her cursed treasure with her.

The wind came up and our galleon drifted back to sea. I have come down this day with a headache. I will not last long."

"That's all there is," said Al, shocked by the story.

"It's a plague ship!" cried Jack. "How long do germs live?"

"The galleon's been floating on the ocean for years and years," said Al, trying to calm himself.

"I don't think it could still be infectious!"

"Run!" shouted Jack, and the children raced from the cabin.

As quickly as they could they ran down to the dory and set sail.

Once they were away from the galleon, Al ordered the sails lowered. He sank them into the water and made a bath, which also acted as a safety net against sharks. "Come on," he said, pointing to the water-filled sails. "We're going to disinfect ourselves."

"What's disinfect?" said Grenda, still bewildered.

"We're having a bath in salt water," explained Hally. "It kills germs."

"Bath?" screeched Grenda. "I've never had a bath."

"You will now," said Al. "We'll take it in turns to go over the side and soak ourselves. Grenda, you're going first and that's an order!"

The Queen

Several days later, with their food supplies running low, Jack sighted land and the rooftops of a large town in the distance.

When they arrived in port they noticed that no one was standing watch on the decks of the boats. The docks were strangely empty and only dogs roamed the streets.

"What's going on?" asked Jack, as the children made their way nervously towards a walled fort nearby.

"Is it a plague city?" whispered Hally.

The fort's gates were shut. Al knocked. His echoing blows eventually summoned a grim guard, who stared at the children in surprise.

"Can you help us?" asked Al. "We've been lost at sea."

"You've come from the sea?" said the guard. A strange, cruel light played in his eyes. "The Queen's prayers have been answered."

Al grabbed Hally's hand, worried by the guard's nasty look.

"Where is everyone?" asked Jack.

"In their homes," the guard replied. "We don't get strangers here and we're having a special day of silence. Your arrival will herald a great ceremony. You must meet our Queen. She'll be delighted you've arrived."

"A queen," repeated Hally. "I'd like to meet a queen."

The guard smiled, showing his teeth. It made Al think of Flash, the awful pirate boy who had stolen his dragon-head ring and who was so false and sneaky.

"Come with me," the guard ordered, "but while we walk through the fort, you're not to speak. Silence must rule today, especially for children." The guard clamped his lips together and led them through hallways hung with pearl-stitched tapestries, until they arrived in a throne room.

More silent guards lined the walls and they waited, stiff-backed, before a pearl-encrusted throne. Beside the throne was a treasure chest piled with more pearls.

"I've never seen so many pearls," whispered Al. "But I don't like the feel of this place at all."

"Shhh!" hissed a guard pushing him in the back. "No one can speak in here unless the Queen says so."

"I can speak," said Hally very loudly. Her voice echoed through the room.

"Because I'm a princess!"

The guard looked slightly surprised and whispered, "In the throne room, children can be seen but must not be heard unless spoken to. Those are the Queen's rules."

A sudden blare of trumpets announced the arrival of a richly veiled woman who was helped onto the throne by servants.

Once seated, the Queen snapped her fingers. A servant arrived holding a glass and a pestle and mortar. The Queen selected some pearls from her treasure chest and dropped them into the earthenware bowl. The servant ground the pearls to dust, tipped it into the glass, then filled the glass with water. The Queen sipped the mixture from behind her veil. Finally, she cleared her throat and beckoned the children closer.

"Where are you from?" she

asked in a thin, frail voice.

"The Dragon Blood Islands," Jack replied as politely as he could. "We were lost at sea and we would like your help."

"Does Vicious Victor still sail the seas?" the Queen asked, ignoring his plea.

"No," said Al, surprised at the question. "He lived a long, long time ago. He's just a legend now."

"Though his ghost still lives on Ghost Island," Hally added. "I saw him once and he was very nice to me. I'm a princess, you see."

There was a long silence from the throne.

"You were not asked to talk," growled the Queen in a voice that sent shivers down Al's spine. "And Vicious Victor was never nice."

"Did you know Vicious Victor?" asked Jack, obviously curious about who was behind the veil.

"Don't be stupid," Grenda interrupted.

"No one's that old. If the Queen knew him she'd be dead."

The Queen cackled, amused by Grenda's words, but then her voice darkened. "You too were told not to speak unless spoken to. Take her away." She flicked her hand angrily and a guard moved forward and took Grenda by the arms.

"I don't think that's very nice," said Hally imperiously. "You shouldn't do that to children. You're very frightening."

The Queen stiffened. A hiss of fury made the guards step back. Goosebumps went down Al's spine. He had a horrible feeling they were in big trouble now.

"Be frightened," the Queen croaked. Slowly she lifted the heavy folds of her veil, revealing wrinkled cheeks studded with pearls, set among weeping boils. Her snarling lips, blue and swollen, were pulled back over long, yellowed teeth. Her eyes flamed from reddened eyeballs. A black diamond hung from a golden chain around her shrivelled neck. "No one argues with me!" She turned to the guards. "They've been sent by the sea god. Now take them to their fate!"

Before Al could protest, the guards hauled the children from the throne room, dragged them down darkened hallways, unlocked a steel door and threw them into a prison cell.

The Prisoners

As Al picked himself up, he saw that the cell was filled with young children.

"Hello," said Hally. "What are you all doing here? Have you been rude to the Queen too?"

The prisoners stared, dumbfounded, at the newcomers. Their pinched faces told Al they were too scared to talk.

"I know the Queen says children should be seen and not heard," said Al, "but we've already been punished. It won't hurt to talk."

"I'll talk," said a small boy. "We've got nothing to lose now. We're doomed."

"Doomed?" asked Al.

"They've caught four of you," said the boy. "That's the number the Queen wanted. Now we're all going to die."

"Die?" exclaimed Jack. "All of you?"

"All of us!" corrected the boy. "There were twenty-six and now there are thirty."

"What's thirty got to do with us dying?" asked Al.

"Every year the Queen sacrifices one of her enemies to the sea monster," another child explained. "But this year she proclaimed that thirty children would be sacrificed instead."

"I've never heard of anything so horrible," cried Hally.

"She's very cruel," piped up a little girl. "My grandmother said that before she came here, we had a good sea god who helped us

find fish and pearls. But this pirate woman came and killed the monks in our temple, and made herself the ruler. Then she and her thugs took over the island, and if anyone disobeys her she throws them to a sea monster. As time went on she said the sea monster was the sea god."

"And now she's the Queen. And she believes if she feeds someone to the monster she'll live for another year," added the small boy.

"It must work," another child said, "because she's still alive."

"But why does she want to feed thirty children to it?" asked Jack.

"The Queen has a witch doctor," said the boy. "A couple of years ago, she decided she wanted to look young again. She said if the doctor didn't make her beautiful she'd feed him to the monster. So he told her to drink pearl dust, but it didn't work. To save his life, the witch doctor told her to sacrifice thirty children – then her beauty would be restored."

"That's unbelievable!" cried Al. "She must be the most stupid evil person in the world!"

"We call her Evil Pearl," the girl agreed. "She kidnapped us before our parents could do anything. We were unlucky – all the other children were hidden by their parents in time. Then she ordered everyone be locked in their houses so no one could rescue us. We hoped she'd never get thirty children but, now you're here, she's done it."

"Any minute we'll be fed to the sea monster," sobbed a young child. "The Queen will waste no time now you're here." With those words the poor prisoners turned their backs on the newcomers, blaming them for their imminent fate.

"I've had enough now," said Hally with a shudder. "I don't want to play princesses any more. I'm scared!"

"So am I," said Grenda, her face pale.

"We can't let being scared stop us from trying to escape," said Al. "We have to think of a way out."

"The Queen loves pearls," said Hally, brightening. "I could offer her my ring." She removed her pearl ring from its hiding place in her dress. "She might swap it for our lives."

"Keep your ring," Grenda advised. "She's

so horrible she'd just take your ring and kill us anyway."

"And we know that the god of the sea isn't the reason she's living forever," added Jack. "Did you see what was hanging from her neck?"

"I think it was a black diamond – given to her by Vicious Victor, I expect," replied Al. "Maybe we could try to tell her about it so

that she would stop feeding people to the sea monster."

"But she wouldn't listen to us – we're just *children*," said Grenda. "I think the only way we'll get out of here is to escape."

"I don't think we've got long before she takes us to the sea monster, though," Jack warned. "Listen."

A steady drumbeat reverberated through the thick walls of the prison. The huddled children began to sob and one cried, "The monster is being called!"

"We have to find a way out of here!" shouted Al, trying to calm everyone.

"We're in a brick room with a steel door," said Jack, looking around their prison. "No windows and no escape."

"There will have been people here before us," Al argued. "Perhaps someone long ago left a clue or something. I reckon we should walk around the room and pat every brick and look out for anything odd. Don't be frightened by the drums, just concentrate on the job."

"What good will that do?" whispered Jack, as the children went to the walls and started patting them.

"It'll keep them busy," said Al, "and stop them being so scared." Then he too turned and began examining the old crumbly walls.

As the drumbeats grew louder Grenda called Al over.

"Look, here!" she said. "There's a message that says, 'You're in danger'. And 'Stop, I wish to talk to you'."

"You can't read," said Al. "How can you see a message?"

"It's a ship's message," said Grenda. "I know what flags say. I just don't know the landlubber squiggles you write on paper."

Al went to Grenda's side and found two flags scratched on the wall.

"Anything else?" asked Al.

"Yes," said Grenda, "there's another flag up there." She pointed high on the wall. "It's so high I can't see it clearly. Maybe someone climbed on someone else's shoulders to write it."

"I'll lift you," said Al. He put his hands down and Grenda stood on his locked palms, then stepped up onto his shoulders. Al straightened and Grenda balanced precariously.

"It says, 'The way is off my ship'," she said.

"Let's push!" shouted Al. "Push the bricks with the flags!"

Grenda pushed and several bricks moved inwards. There was a cry of joy as a small tunnel was revealed.

Within minutes, Al organised a pyramid of people, with Al, Grenda, Hally and Jack on the bottom and the smaller children on the top. Then Al sent the biggest boy to climb up. He scrambled into the tunnel and pulled one of the other children inside. One by one the children disappeared into the tunnel.

Then, just as Grenda, Hally, Al and Jack were organising themselves to climb up, the drums stopped. They could hear footsteps.

"They're coming," said Jack. "We won't have time to escape."

"We can't let them find the others," said Al. "If there's no longer thirty of us then the ceremony will be delayed. It would buy us all time."

"Put the bricks back so they can't find you," Jack called up to the other children, who were now safe in the tunnel.

Seconds later, just as the bricks were

replaced, the prison door was flung open. The mystified guards grabbed the four remaining children and dragged them outside.

Monster from the Sea

The four shipmates soon found themselves
inside a temple built over the ocean. Men
standing beside large drums waited next to
a dark pool of water. On an old-looking
platform, jutting into the pool, stood Evil
Pearl. "Where are the others?" she croaked,
seeing only four victims.

"The other children have vanished!"
cried a guard, falling to his knees before the

Queen. "Only these four were inside the prison. The very four that came to us from the sea!"

"It was the sea god's will!" cried another terrified guard.

Pearl stiffened in rage. "I need thirty children," she hissed. "But now the sea god has been called and he's hungry and waiting. He must be fed. These children alone will have to do this time. We can get others later." She raised her hand and, on the command, the drum roll sounded.

The water beside her churned in response. A colourless head, three metres high and at least two metres wide, erupted from the waters. Two basketball-sized eyes, yellow like a cat's, focused on the children. The monstrous creature shivered expectantly, waiting for a signal to feed, as several tentacles squirmed in the water.

"It's a giant squid!" whispered Jack.

"Queen Pearl!" Al cried desperately. "Please don't feed us to the monster. The black diamond around your neck is what makes you live so long, not the sea god."

The Queen turned and pointed a gnarled finger at Al. "By speaking, you have chosen to be the first sacrifice," she growled. The drumbeat grew faster and louder as a guard dragged Al towards the squid.

Fear for her brother gave Hally unexpected strength. She kicked her guard's ankle, broke free from his grip and stepped towards the evil Queen, holding out her pearl ring. "Take it!" she cried. "Take it and let my brother live."

A cackling laugh escaped from the Queen's throat. "I'll have the ring *and* your brother's life," she threatened. She turned to the guard. "Get her," she ordered. "Take her ring and feed her to the sea god with her brother."

She waved her hand again and the beating drums stopped.

The giant squid's slimy tentacles lashed out, grabbed Al and squeezed him with their bruising suckers. In the terrifying silence, the creature slowly pulled Al towards its mouth. Its giant beak snapped eagerly, ready to tear him limb from limb.

Hally fought as the guard caught her

wrists. "How dare you!" she shouted at the Queen. "How dare you hurt us! I wish your disgusting squid would leave my brother alone. And I wish someone would punish you for all the nasty things you've done!"

At her fierce words, Hally's magical pearl ring lit up, as if it was a mirror with sunlight hitting it. It flashed with such fire that it reflected in the squid's eyes. The creature shuddered slightly. Some grain of thought registered in its primordial brain. Its tentacles loosened and Al was unexpectedly set free.

The squid fixed its hungry yellow eyes on Hally as the guard dragged her towards the squid. "Leave me alone!" Hally cried. "I wish you'd leave me alone!"

The ring flashed again. Suddenly the hungry squid's tentacles whipped and whirled around Hally's head, while Evil Pearl snatched the ring from her captive's hand.

Just as suddenly, the giant squid grabbed

the Queen. An ear-splitting shriek sent
goosebumps down Al's spine as Evil Pearl was
lifted into the air.

The wicked woman flailed and punched
at the rubbery tentacles that encircled her.
She bit and kicked viciously, enraging the
squid. Another tentacle shot from the water,
snaking around her. The giant creature

squeezed tighter and tighter and, holding Evil
Pearl in a death grip, it dragged her struggling
and screaming into the water.

Horrified, Al reached out and held his
sobbing sister. They stood together, watching
the seething water below. Al shivered with
dread; he knew the squid couldn't kill Pearl.
She wore the black diamond! She also had

Hally's ring which, he realised too late, had power over sea creatures. The jewels would keep her alive no matter what the squid did to her.

Al stood locked in fear, knowing Evil Pearl could emerge from the water at any moment. Even if she was horribly damaged, she could still hurt them.

Suddenly, behind Al and Hally, the doors to the temple burst open. Angry villagers bearing rakes and spades rushed into the room and quickly overpowered the guards.

It seemed that the imprisoned children had crawled through the escape tunnel, found their way home and begged

their parents to help the newcomers who had rescued them. Furious about the treatment of their children, the parents had gathered together and headed for the temple.

But Al was still so worried that Evil Pearl would return from the ocean that he was oblivious to the commotion behind him. Fearfully, he searched the waters, until a shimmer of gold caught his eye. Something was caught on a rusty nail just below him. Nervously, he bent over and unhooked…a necklace!

"She must be dead!" he cried, holding the Queen's black diamond high. "Evil Pearl is gone!"

Safe and Sound

Later that day, Al, Hally, Grenda and Jack were treated to a party, and thanked hundreds of times. The children's mothers wore them out with kisses and cuddles, and asked them what they would like as a reward.

They didn't have to think twice. They asked for provisions so they could return to sea and find Snotty Nell.

It wasn't long before they were ready to leave. As they climbed into their boat, the grateful islanders gave them each a bag of shining pearls in thanks.

Several days later, far out at sea, Al sighted a ship glowing deep copper in the sunlight. A fine skull and crossbones flew at the mast.

"It's *The Invincible*!" exclaimed Jack, as Al tacked towards it.

"Captain Gunner!" Al called, as *The Invincible* hove to, and Gunner lowered a ladder.

"Look! There's Snakeboot, sitting on the rails," shouted Hally, waving. "I love that cat! And there's Mahoot. I haven't seen him in ages."

"Grenda!" Captain Gunner roared back. "What are you doing here? And Hally, where did you come from?"

"We've had such an adventure!" Jack yelled.

"But we're so glad to see you. And…" he held up the pearls, "…we've got treasure!"

Over a dinner in the galley, Gunner and Mahoot listened open-mouthed to what had happened to Al, Jack, Hally and Grenda.

Al was wracking his brains about how to explain Hally's presence, when Gunner said, "Well, young Al, you're a rascal of a whippersnapper. You told me you didn't know how the sabre and scabbard worked, but I know Hally couldn't have got to Sabre Island on her own, because you left her in town ages ago! So how do you explain her getting to Sabre Island? There was no sign of her when we were there last."

Al reddened and looked at Jack for help. How could he tell Gunner they lived in the twenty-first century and had fallen into the ocean after stepping through a magical sea trunk?

"I can see you're going red," Gunner said,

"so I'm gunner answer for you." He tapped
his nose knowingly, and lowered his voice.
"I think you've learnt how to use the sabre.
You hid it with your sister in town, and she
used it to get to Sabre Island. Then you got
caught by the tide and washed out to sea!"
He slapped Al heartily on the back. "Now,
isn't that the truth?"

Al looked at Jack again. Jack shrugged, so
Al nodded, feeling guilty at the white lie, but
knowing it was the easiest option.

"I thought so," said Gunner. "I'm not
stupid, you know. But if we want to get the
sabre back we're gunner have to trade Grenda
for it." He smiled at Grenda. "I'm sure you
won't mind helping us get the sabre back by
being a hostage."

After searching the ocean for several days, the
Nausi VIII's sails were sighted near Mermaid
Island.

Vampire Zu, who was still at the *Nausi VIII*'s helm, couldn't believe his eyes as Gunner's boat bore down on them, closed in as if for battle, and then raised its white flag. He trained his telescope on the approaching ship, expecting a trick, and spied Grenda at the prow. He hove to, with all guns aimed at *The Invincible*. "Fetch the captain," he ordered. "Gunner's got Grenda!"

Snotty leapt from her bunk, dried her weepy eye, wiped her top lip and hobbled onto the deck.

"Give me back my daughter," Snotty screamed, "or I'll rip your heart out and dance to its beat!"

"You're outgunned!" Gunner yelled back. "And since I've got Grenda, behave yourself, Booger Face."

"What do you want?" Snotty yelled.

"Give back the sabre and scabbard you stole," Gunner called.

A dark smile hovered on Snotty's lips. "Gunner doesn't know it's a fake," she whispered to Vampire, "but if I give it up too easily, he'll be suspicious."

"It's not enough!" she cried out to her adversary. "I'm sailing a horrible wallowing pig of a boat because of you. What I have here is the most valuable treasure in all the Dragon Blood Islands, so I want some gold as well."

Grenda was surprised and saddened by her mother's reply. "It's as if she doesn't care about me at all," she said with a sigh.

"I think she's afraid of looking weak in front of her crew," Gunner said kindly.

"Well, tell her you'll give her a bag of pearls," said Grenda. "She can have mine. I was going to give them to her as a surprise anyway."

"We can throw in a bag of fine pearls!" Gunner yelled. "And if you don't accept, I'm gunner slit your daughter's gizzard and feed her to Greeny Joe."

"You drive a hard bargain, you sea scoundrel," Snotty called back. "But we'll make the swap!"

An hour later, Grenda was safely in her mother's arms and Snotty had reassured her daughter why she had demanded more treasure.

Happy, but still trying to avoid another kiss and slobber on her cheek, Grenda told her mother about sneaking onto Mermaid Island, the horror of the black diamond and the terrible Evil Pearl.

"So they weren't fakes after all," said Snotty. "You know, I nearly made the diamonds on the scabbard into earrings." She shuddered. "I wouldn't want to be cursed like Pearl." She hugged her daughter again. "I'm so glad you're safe and sound. You're

the only treasure I really care about. I'd hate
to outlive the ones I love. I'm glad those
horrible boys have the curse with them."

That night, on board *The Invincible*, with
Snakeboot purring on his cushion in the
children's cabin, Mahoot asked, "Have
you really learnt how the sabre works?
Grandfather will be overjoyed!"

Al shook his head. "I'm afraid we haven't,"

he sighed. "There's other magic at work that we still don't understand."

"And I've had quite enough of it," said Hally. Tears sprang to her eyes. "I'm going to have nightmares for weeks."

Mahoot looked at Hally with concern. "I'll go and make you a cup of hot soup," he said. "You look like you could do with one."

When Mahoot had gone to the galley, Hally sobbed on Al's shoulder. "I want to go

home now," she said. "I wish I was in my safe, warm bed."

Snakeboot jumped down from his cushion. His ghostly purple eyes gleamed. Without any warning Al's arms and legs began to tingle. He looked across at Jack and Hally, who were shimmering and fading too.

"Oh no!" Al cried. "We're going home. Right here, right now."

Seconds later he found himself standing in his attic at number five Drake Drive in the twenty-first century, with Jack and Hally beside him.

Mahoot and Captain Gunner soon returned to the cabin carrying cups of soup. Snakeboot was purring on his cushion, but the children were gone.

"There really is a mystery here," said Mahoot to Gunner. "I know only one person can fly with the sabre – not three. Something else must be happening."

"Aha!" cried Gunner. "I told you. They know how to use the sabre and they've flown off somewhere. They'd better return soon and show me how to use it!"

Captain's Code

Can you decipher the following message
written with maritime flags? Check out
www.dragonbloodpirates.co.uk for the keys
to the Captain's Code…if you dare!

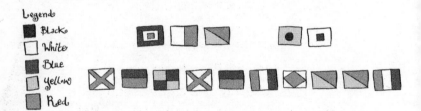

Legend
- ■ Black
- □ White
- ■ Blue
- ■ Yellow
- ■ Red

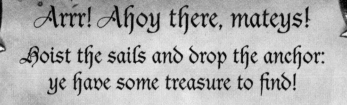

Arrr! Ahoy there, mateys!

Hoist the sails and drop the anchor: ye have some treasure to find!

One swashbucklin' reader will win an ipod Touch and ten runners up will win a Dragon Blood Pirates booty bag. For a chance to win, ye must dare to unearth the treasure!

Each of the six **Dragon Blood Pirates: The Legend of Dragon Island** books contain a clue.
When you have solved the six clues, enter the answers online at www.dragonbloodpirates.co.uk

Or send your name, address and answers to:

Dragon Blood Pirates:
The Legend of Dragon Island
338 Euston Road, London NW1 3BH

Best o' luck, me hearties!

To find where the pirate treasure lies,
ye must find the answer to the clue that lies below:

**This ship is owned by a snivelling pirate,
Who maroons our heroes in a terrible climate.**

www.dragonbloodpirates.co.uk

Ahoy there shipmates!

To reel in amazin' pirate booty, steer smartly
towards www.dragonbloodpirates.co.uk

Ye'll find games, downloads, activities and
sneak previews of the latest swashbucklin'
Dragon Blood Pirates adventures.
Learn how to speak all pirate-like, how to find
out what type of pirate ye be, an' what pirate
games ye can play with yer mates! This treasure
trove is a sure feast fer yer deadlights!

Only the bravest an' heartiest amon' ye
can become a true scurvy dog, so don't
ye miss a thing and sign up to yer newsletter
at www.dragonbloodpirates.co.uk!

Don't ye miss book eleven in the

Dragon Blood Pirates

series!

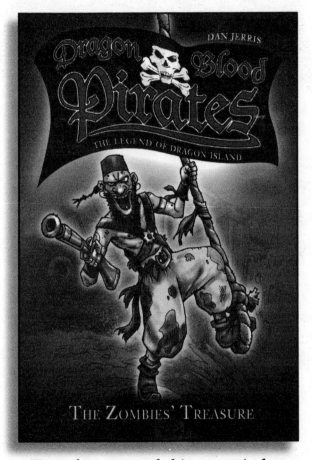

Turn the page and shiver yer timbers
with a slice of the next high-seas adventure…

Return to the Dragon Blood Islands

"We've collected three black diamonds for the Scabbard of Invincibility," said Al Breas, holding up a silver sheath. "Now there's only one more to find before it will get legendary powers."

"Then, when you wear it, you'll be invincible," said Jack Seabrook, Al's best friend. "We need to go back to the

Dragon Blood Islands."

"Yep, I agree," said Al.

"Great! Are we going to take the Dragon Blood Sabre and scabbard this time?" asked Jack.

Al thought for a few moments before answering. "I'd rather not," he said. "If a pirate sees them we'll be in trouble, and I'm not invincible yet, just deathless." He shuddered slightly.

"Why don't we just take our chances?" said Jack, realising his friend was worried about it.

"I suppose," said Al. "I keep having horrible thoughts about wearing it. Like I'm alive but my head is missing, or my gizzards are ripped out and I have to try to stitch them back in. This whole deathless thing gives me the creeps. Who'd want to be like Razor Toe and Evil Pearl?"

"I'm not so keen on the deathless thing

either," Jack agreed. "They were horrible. Just thinking about them makes me want to vomit."

"I wonder where the final diamond is…" said Al. "Maybe there's some other ancient old pirate out there causing trouble?"

"Or it could be at the bottom of the sea so we'll never find it," said Jack with a chuckle. "I think we should just go back to have a bit of fun. I can't wait to see Mahoot and Gunner again."

"They're probably wondering how we disappeared from *The Invincible* so suddenly," said Al. "I'm sure Gunner thinks I used the Dragon Blood Sabre, and that we don't trust him."

"We could try telling him the truth," said Jack, hesitantly.

"Let's get changed then, and see if we can find him," said Al. "Who knows, we might end up on Sabre Island and go swimming with the elephants again," Jack said with a sparkle in his eyes.

Several minutes later the boys were dressed in their pirate clothes, ready to leave the twenty-first century and Al's home at number five Drake Drive.

Al took a key from a hook, unlocked an old sea trunk that had a map of the Dragon Blood Islands painted on its base, and took a deep breath. As he stepped into the trunk a familiar tingling went up through his feet and carried to his fingers. He became transparent, the air glowed mysteriously and he vanished. Jack stepped in behind his friend, wondering where they would land this time.

The Warning Bell

Al and Jack had landed somewhere so dark they could barely see their hands in front of their eyes. A heaving swell under their feet and a heavy night sky above told them they were at sea, on a ship, but the eerie tolling of a bell confused them. Bells were usually found in churches, weren't they — not on the waves?

A pallid shape looming out of the dark near the boat's rails attracted their attention.

Al stepped closer and found himself staring into the empty eye sockets of a skull. "This isn't good," he whispered. "Not good at all."

More lifeless faces peered back at them from the walls of a small cabin. "There are skulls everywhere!" gulped Jack, the hairs rising on his neck.

"Let's keep away from the cabin," said Al. "Somebody nasty could be sleeping there. Let's move towards the bow."

The boys climbed down a stairway that led to an open hull fitted with rowing benches. "It's like a giant rowboat," said Jack, as they clambered over the oars.

"At least fifty people would be needed to row this ship," observed Al. "But it's empty. What's a rowing boat doing out in the middle of the ocean? And why does that bell keep ringing?"

"It's like a slave galley, but with no slaves," said Jack. "And there are more skulls nailed beside every set of oars."

"Maybe the ringing is a ship's bell," said Al hopefully. "If it's another ship nearby, we might be able to get off this spooky boat."

The boys stood on tiptoe and peered over the bowsprit into the night. Not far away a lantern shone from a small rowboat, illuminating a man rowing away from the galley. He moved purposefully towards a bell mounted on a raft. The bell tolled with each wave, and the boys realised it was warning of razor-sharp rocks jutting from the ocean.

"What's the guy in the dinghy doing?" asked Jack, as the man climbed onto the raft.

The ocean swell lifted the boys high and they lost vision for a minute. Seconds later the mighty bell rang again. When the raft came back into sight, a knife glinted as the man hacked the bell's supporting ropes. With a mighty clang the bell plunged into the waters.

"What did he do that for?" asked Jack.

"I guess we'll find out," said Al, "because he's heading back here."

"But we don't want him to find us!" said Jack. He tapped a grinning skull beside him. "I don't want to end up like that. We'd better hide, quickly."

It didn't take the boys long to find supply boxes covered with canvas, near the prow. Beside the boxes were several large water barrels, lashed against the hull, hiding a space made by the hull's wooden ribs. Al and Jack ducked behind the barrels, squeezing themselves into the gap with their backs against the wall. It was uncomfortable, but they had a line of sight all the way up the boat to the cabin.

A bump against the side of the ship and the slither of ropes told the boys the lone rower had returned – and he was lashing the rowboat to the galley.

Shipwreck

The day broke with a fresh wind that tossed the galley on its anchor. The man who had cut the bell from the raft sat cross-legged on the deck in front of his cabin.

Al squirmed in his hiding place, trying to make the blood move in his legs. He was wondering if he should crawl out and announce his presence – he could no longer stand the wood pressing into every part of his body. But suddenly the man stood up. He shuffled down the stairs and through the rowing benches towards the water barrel. Red velvet slippers muffled his footsteps.

With heavily jewelled hands he lifted the lid of the water barrel, only inches from Al's nose, and collected a cup hanging from a string. "Arggh," he grunted, as he slurped the water and licked his lips, "there'll be a storm by nightfall." He chuckled and tapped a skull nailed above the barrel. A gold ring with a large black diamond flashed in the sunlight. Al's heart lurched in his chest at the sight.

"And so, old ship mate," the man continued, addressing the skull. "Ye'll be a-grinning, 'cause another capt'n will be a-rowing in yer old place soon enough. For the storm'll bring Velvetfoot a new crew.

And ye were a great old capt'n, were ye not! Ye gave old Velvetfoot many a good treasure." He chuckled, replaced the cup on the nail, turned and went silently back to his cabin.

The sea rose higher, crashing onto the nearby rocks, and the galley seesawed on its anchor. The wind tossed darkening clouds, and Al's legs cramped painfully.

"It's getting very rough," whispered Jack. "I'm in agony. I can't stand it any longer. I think I'd rather risk death."

"Wait!" Al pleaded. "I saw a black diamond on the man's hand! It's too dangerous. Maybe tonight, while he's sleeping, we can take his rowboat and escape."

By night Al's stomach was grumbling with hunger, his bottom was numb and a storm was making conditions unbearable.

Finally, when it was late and no light came from the cabin, he dared to make a move.

"Let's try to get out of here," he whispered to Jack, as he dragged himself from his hiding place and slithered out into the hull on his stomach. Jack followed, pulling himself from his hidey-hole.

They were lying on their backs, rubbing their aching arms and legs, when a loud *bang!* startled them into sitting up. The strong wind brought a sickening crash of wood grinding over rocks, the booming of sails as they were backed in the wind and then the shriek of tearing canvas. This was followed by shouts of disbelief and fear from men in danger of drowning.

"Someone's hit the rocks in the storm," said Al. "They'll sink! What'll we do?"

As if in answer, there was a flash of light from Velvetfoot's cabin. Velvetfoot shuffled to the rails, then to his dinghy, carrying a lantern and a blunderbuss.

The boys raced to their vantage point

at the prow and watched as, in the raging
spume of waves, a small trading boat was
smashed against the reef.

Velvetfoot rowed towards the boat and
waited till a longboat was lowered from it by
ropes, which the crew would use to escape
their sinking vessel. When the life-saving boat
was halfway to the water, Velvetfoot fired his
blunderbuss. The ropes burst apart, sending
the longboat crashing into the turbulent sea.

Several men fell with it. Velvetfoot rowed towards one of the floundering men and hauled him from the water, before rowing him back to the galley.

Once aboard, Velvetfoot led the man, at the point of his blunderbuss, to the cabin. He brought out a dark blue bottle and ordered the survivor to drink.

Within seconds, the rescued man fell senseless to the deck. Velvetfoot rolled him to one side and returned to his dinghy.

The crew of the broken-backed trading boat stood miserably by the gunnels, gazing at the murderous sea slowly destroying their longboat – and their chance of escape.

Velvetfoot rowed towards the stricken vessel. "Throw old Velvetfoot a rope!" he called. "I'll save your hides, but Velvetfoot's rowboat can only carry one at a time. Have patience and Velvetfoot'll save you all!"

One at a time, he brought the men to

his galley and urged them to drink, and by daybreak, more than fifty lay unconscious at the stern. Jack and Al could only watch in horror.

In the pre-dawn light the pirate skull and crossbones flew above the shredded sail of the wrecked trading boat. Jack and Al realised they knew this ship – and its captain! They soon saw the last man lowering himself into Velvetfoot's tossing dinghy. Sure enough, it was Blacktooth.

As soon as Blacktooth was in the boat, Velvetfoot ordered him to drink. Blacktooth swigged from the blue bottle and slumped forward.

"I don't think Velvetfoot knows who he's dealing with," whispered Jack. "When the pirates wake up they'll take over the galley. Velvetfoot can't fight them all…"